Welcome to our 6th Hailsham Festival Anthology

This year our usual Creative Writing competitions asked for short stories title "The Dinner Party" and poems title "Moon". This brought in some amazing creative ideas on both subjects. I have started the book with the Moon entries, followed by the short stories. After these, you will find a selection of writing that came over to me with no desire to go into the competitions, so I have included them for you to see also.

The children have not come forward in great numbers again, but you will find 3 short stories entitled "On the Beach" and 2 poems with the name "My pet".
Creative Writing has always been an essential part of the Hailsham Festival of Arts and Culture and I hope it will always continue to be so.

I have enjoyed my part in this activity and would like to say that I had 3 independent judges for these competitions and all entries were submitted to them without any identification of the writer.

Thank you for your support for Hailsham Festival in buying this publication.

Keep writing…!

Pam Robinson
Editor

Cover photo:

The Artists' Bridge, Hailsham, formerly Eastwell Pace Bridge.

The Artists' Bridge in Hailsham, East Sussex (Eastwell Place Bridge) was opened on September 9th 2023 as part of Hailsham Festival of Arts and Culture. The bridge crosses the disused railway track which is now an attractive trail for walkers and cyclists known as the Cuckoo Trail. The bridge had been somewhat unloved for a number of years and was frequently covered in unwelcome graffiti. The bridge now features over 75 pieces of art submitted by local artists and is enjoyed by the people of Hailsham.

Photo: Richard Goldsmith

All rights strictly reserved. No part of this publication may be reproduced, stored in a retrievable system, or transmitted at any time by any means, electronic, mechanical, photocopying, recording or otherwise, without prior permission of the copyright holder.
© For this volume resides with the Hailsham Festival of Arts and Culture.
© For each piece resides with each individual author. Authors may be contacted through the Hailsham Festival website contacts' link.

All opinions, thoughts and ideas contained in this book are those of the individual author and may not represent those of the Anthology editor or Hailsham Festival Committee.

Table of Contents

Cover photo: 2

Viki Allerston   9
    The Dinner Party

Janet Wilkinson   11
    The Dinner Party

Julie Bradley   14
    The Dinner Party

Helene Ford   16
    The Dinner Party (The Easter Offering)

Maggie Jakins   18
    The Dinner Party

Jacky Long   20
    The Dinner Party

Mike Daws   23
    The Dinner Party

Heather Suart   26
    The Dinner Party

Diane Newman   29
    The Dinner Party

Donna Ripley   31
    The Dinner Party

Jennifer de Grey   34
    The Dinner Party

Chris Caudron   37
    The Dinner Party

Yvette P. Rejuso — 40
    The Dinner Party

Rebecca Clifford — 42
    After the Wolf Blood Moon

Sarah Wooler — 43
    The Moon

Debbie Milner — 44
    The Reflecting Moon

Heather Suart — 45
    The Moon

Jennifer de Grey — 46
    Moon

Teresa Fowler — 47
    Moon

Donna Ripley — 48
    Moon

Rebecca Clifford — 49
    I See the Moon

Rebecca Clifford — 50
    I See

Sue Ribbons — 51
    Moon

Mike Daws — 53
    Moon

(The Man in The Moon) — 53

Chris Ralls — 54
    Moon

Loraine Banks	55
Moon	
Diane Newman	56
Poem 'Moon'	
Chris Caudron	57
Moon	
Leanne Pilbeam	58
Moon Cheese	
Bohhdan Rafalskyi	59
My Pet	
Sebby Smith (aged 6)	61
My Pet	
Ned Rollo (aged 10)	62
On the Beach	
George Rollo (aged 10)	63
On the Beach	
Harry Saunders (aged 10)	64
On the Beach	
Maggie Jakins	65
Plugged In	
Pam Robinson	67
Where next......?	
Pam Robinson	70
Tea is served...	
Harry Saunders (aged 10)	71
The Cavemen	

Harry Saunders (10)   *72*
    The Time Travellers
Gail Landon   *73*
    Today Veyra Rules
Creative Writing Competitions - Winners   *75*

Viki Allerston

The Dinner Party

Betty loved giving Dinner Parties, seeing friends sitting around her big circular table. It seated nine comfortably, eight guests and herself.

She beamed at tonight's collection. Ted, a really cuddly sort, loved by everyone. The one tiny problem was his tendency to tip sideways. Betty always discreetly nudged him upright as she passed with cups and plates. No-one seemed to notice.

Next to him was one-time Michael, when he had short hair. But with a shoulder-length wig, red nails and lips he was now known as Michaela.

Beside him/her was Charlie. With his red nose, raised eye-brows and forever smiling mouth, he made everyone happy and laughing and was consequently known as 'Charlie Clown.'

Then there were the twins, Susie and Sonia. They had co-joined hands, Sonia's left attached to Susie's right. Consequently they both needed a little help with cups and food. As Betty circled the table offering plates, she was careful to return in the opposite direction, ensuring neither thought the other was receiving greater consideration.

Next was Bridget. She had come from Ireland and with huge blue eyes, creamy skin and dark hair, was beautiful. Her long white dress, flowery headband that had once held a small veil, earned her the nick-name of Bridie.

Her cream skin off-set the black skin of Sam, next to her. He had never objected to being known as Sambo, but as it was no longer PC he was now Sam.

On the seat between Sam and herself was Rosebud. A cherubic little face, rosebud mouth, her dark hair holding a small pink bow. Her dress with its puffed sleeves, full skirt, covered with a rose-bud design, completed the picture, meaning she was aptly named.

Betty herself was plump and motherly. Born in 1964, the same year as Boris Johnson, she couldn't help but wonder that had he had friends like hers at those fateful parties, he could have spared himself the appalling fall from grace.

Looking at the amount of food still on the plates stacked in the kitchen, she estimated there was enough there to last her three days.

Even so, she was very relieved things were back to normal. She looked forward to giving her next Dinner Party to gossiping, noisy humans instead of using her childhood toys as guests.

Janet Wilkinson

The Dinner Party

Finley and his great aunty Lizzy were having fun racing two remote controlled vehicles round his grandad's large garden. Finley was playing with a new monster truck and Lizzy was playing with an old sports car that used to belong to Finley's great uncle Jed.

Lizzy and Jed had given Finley the monster truck and the old sports car which was still in good order. The monster truck was great for climbing over the rockery and the sports car sped round the paths at great speed. Finley was having a good time.

Although it was not his birthday Finlay was having a dinner party as a special celebration. Two weeks ago everyone attending this dinner party had received a text message telling them Finlay had rung the bell at the hospital which signalled he was on his way home.

He had finished his chemotherapy and was enjoying life again. The rest of his treatment for leukaemia was to be in the form of a daily dose of banana flavoured medicine.

"Yuck," Finley had said to the nurse who gave him his first dose. "Please ask the doctor if I can have chemo instead." He soon got used to the medicine.

Finlay's immediate family and a few of his friends had joined him at his grandad's house today and while grandad and his great uncles were in the lounge watching Leicester Tigers playing in the rugby cup final on television, Finley, his great aunty Lizzy and his friends were all having fun in the garden.

Suddenly there was loud cheering from the lounge. The Tigers had scored the winning goal in the last minute of the match.

Finley's mum, Emma called everyone in from the garden and led them into the dining room where a wonderful feast was waiting for them.

Everyone sat down and Finley rang the dinner gong to say they could start eating.

There was a lot of chatter round the table as they enjoyed their meal.

The conversation turned to names and why everyone had more than one name they were known by. Finley asked his great uncle Jed why he had several names.

Jed explained his real name of Jeremy is the one given to him by his mum and dad when he was born. His two sisters call him James and his brother, who is Finley's grandad calls him Jame. All his morris dancing friends know him as Jed.

"That is very confusing," said Finley, "what should I call you Uncle Jed?"

"You can call me anything you like," said Jed. "As I have no hair you can call me baldy if you want," said Jed, rubbing the top of his head.

Finley laughed and thought about it for a few minutes as he stared at Jed's wrinkled leathery face.

"I know," he said finally. "I will call you Uncle Blue Eyes."

Everyone agreed Uncle Blue Eyes was a lovely name to add to the list of names Jed was known by.

Julie Bradley

The Dinner Party

"Oh no" exclaimed Mabel as she looked at the card in her hand "Johnny look at this, we are invited to dinner at the Trubshaws on Saturday". Johnny's head shot up from the paper he was reading "Oh God, not the Trubshaws – that's always a fun night, I guess we will have to go though or we will never hear the last of it". Mabel sighed and pulled a face "Well we have got a week to prepare ourselves Johnny"
Mabel always dreaded the Trubshaws dinners. Daphne and Michael were old school – very Victorian and formal – and their dinners were very boring. However Johnny and Mabel were always invited as the men were golfing buddies.
The dreaded day arrived and Mabel and Johnny were decked out in their finery. Johnny in black tie and Mabel in a dark blue evening dress which glittered in the light. They had ordered a taxi so that Johnny could partake in some of the copious amounts of alcohol that was always supplied.
They arrived at the Trubshaws large house and were greeted by the maid at the door and escorted into the lounge.
Daphne Trubshaw trotted over to them "Lovely to see you again" she warbled, her several chins wobbling as she spoke. She was a large lady and was dressed in a vibrant red dress which accentuated her curves. Michael was a fairly dapper man somewhat eclipsed by

his large wife but they seemed happy enough in their formal ways. "Johnny old man come and help me with the drinks and we will leave the girls to chat" Michael said as he strolled across. Mabel groaned inwardly and tried to look interested.

The dinner gong sounded and everyone trooped into the dining room. Mabel was seated between Michael and old Major Williams. He always ended up with food clinging to his vast moustache which amused Mabel. Johnny had drawn the short straw and was placed between Daphne and Eileen Roberts, another pompous and loud octogenarian. He sighed and wished the evening would go quickly.

Dinner was served. The wine flowed and the talk became louder. Suddenly there was a gasp and a loud crash and Daphne Trubshaw fell backwards with her legs in the air as her chair shattered under her weight. Everyone froze. She lay there for a moment with a shocked look on her face unable to move. Johnny who was sat next to her looked across at Mabel who was trying not to laugh. Suddenly the room erupted as everyone rushed to Daphne's aid. "Oh dear" she said as she was helped up "We must get that chair looked at, there was obviously a fault somewhere". She was not hurt, another chair was found and dinner continued as before.

"Well that was interesting" laughed Mabel as they made their way home. "Poor old Daphne – bet she is upset about everyone getting a look at her underwear" replied Johnny "It certainly livened the evening up"!

Helene Ford

The Dinner Party (The Easter Offering)

Because the vicar received the Easter Offering each year it was the custom for the vicar and his wife to entertain the parishioners to supper at the vicarage. However it was different this year, because the vicar and his wife were retiring and going to live in another parish. Evelyn wasn't sorry to be leaving the vicarage. It was draughty, expensive to heat and maintenance in recent years had been sadly lacking.
Evelyn wondered why it was perfectly acceptable for the vicar's wife to be wielding a paint brush and skiving in the vicarage, but not in a member of the congregation's house when those people had far more disposable income than she herself would ever have or would ever see.
Invitations had been sent out, shopping done and the vicarage received it's spring clean.
Last time, muttered Evelyn s she flicked the feather duster under Chris's chin.
One of the recipients of an invitation was Mary the farmer's daughter who lived next door; Mary was raising an orphan lamb but he was now quickly growing into an adult sheep. Like the nursery rhyme, everywhere that Mary went the lamb was sure to go.
Then, days before the Easter celebrations, a strange thing happened in the village. Parcels of lamb began appearing, tied to people's gate posts. The sisters who were the oldest residents received a lovely leg. Mrs Jones the post

mistress some chunky chops and the Doctor another leg.

When Mary's lamb did not appear for his supper Mary went in search. He had got through a gap in the hedge and was nowhere to be found. Given the fact that the village had been showered with parcels of lamb. Mary was beside herself.

Reluctantly, Mary was persuade to go to the vicarage supper. When the vicar sharpened the carving knife and the joint of lamb was carried into the dining room Mary could take no more. She got up and rushed from the room. Faced with eating her beloved pet Mary's heart was broken.

Reaching the farmhouse door, Mary turned and there stood her lamb waiting for his supper. She was overjoyed, but she also knew that it was time for he lamb to join the flock. Sadly Mary took her lamb to the fields where the sheep were. Knowing that next year she would probably be called again to help again. As for the Mystery of the lamb presents, the puzzle was never solved. The gifts were however gratefully received.

Maggie Jakins

The Dinner Party

It was the perfect start to the evening; there had been plenty of rain all day. For the vegetarians, and of those there were many, the menu was to die for - fresh young peas, juicy bean shoots, and a variety of mixed salads. The guests needed no invitation, the slugs always being the first to arrive, closely followed by their cousins, the snails. No call for knives and forks, or even plates, at *this* dinner party. Every damp-loving creature of the night was well-equipped to enjoy a sumptuous feast under the cover of darkness. They were all nicely rested, having spent the day tucked under upturned flowerpots or clinging to the shed door, out of sight of sharp-beaked birds and the gardener's fork.
Like a silent army, the gastropods slid and crept their way across the vegetable patch, leaving tell-tale trails in their wake, munching their way through tender shoots and newly sprouted leaves.
'Be careful as you pass the pond,' a cautious snail reminded. 'There's been a mean frog under that broken pot every night this week with nothing better to do than lie in wait for us.'
'Let's head over to the buffet,' a young slug said excitedly. 'I can smell fresh marigolds.'
'I'll see you there later,' a caterpillar replied. 'It's a bit of a tricky climb, but I so prefer the taste of sprouts and I simply adore making holes in the leaves, darling. They look like

fancy lace curtains when I've finished – fabulous.'

'Be careful,' a passing worm warned. 'Don't go snacking on those little blue pellets. Brian got such an upset stomach after eating some last week. Haven't seen him around since…'

The uninvited guests made short work of fresh young shoots, leaving just enough stalk in the damp ground to snack on later. One or two of the more adventurous types edged their way carefully up the bean poles, enticed by the bright red flowers nodding in the night air.

'Please tell me they've re-stocked those seedlings,' said a latecomer as she took her place around the selection of lettuces. 'They're my favourite, lovely and juicy,' and they all nodded in agreement, too busy devouring the treats to engage in dinner party small talk.

Dawn was beginning to glow up the sky – the sign for guests to leave the dinner party before the sun dried everything around. The fat and full began slithering back under the flowerpots to seek shade from the rising sun.

One or two slugs paused on their way home, to shake their heads at those who had indulged in the shallow tray of beer that was thoughtfully refreshed for them every night, although the revellers no longer seemed active.

'Same time tomorrow then?' a sleepy slug asked no-one in particular as he curled himself into a satisfied ball under the water butt.

'Oh yes, count me in,' a snail replied. 'But that was the best dinner party ever.'

Jacky Long

The Dinner Party

The care home where Jo works, sits alongside the river in the desirable village of Sonning. Tomorrow is Jo's birthday 'Maybe I'll take the day off from the home. Maybe I'll do something different this year to my usual Chinese takeaway' she muses. 'Maybe I'll have a party!' The trouble is, Jo has few friends. 'I could invite the launderette assistant or the woman I feed ducks with on a Wednesday.'

'Where to have this party?' she wonders. 'My bedsit is probably not ideal. Bit too, you know, cosy. Be better to have my party out somewhere.' Jo's imagination is firing up. 'I know! Chips with wooden forks sitting by the river, maybe even mushy peas too. I'm only 50 once!'

Invitations dispatched, Jo wakes up on her birthday, quite excited about the notion of her party on the banks of the Thames. 6pm arrives and so do Jo's guests. The addition of the mushy peas to the menu appears to be appreciated, judging by the audible 'oohs' and 'aahs'.

Suddenly this genial supper is interrupted by a passing gentleman. 'Are you Jo from the care home?' he asks. Jo nods in the affirmative, bemused as she doesn't recognise the man.

'I thought I recognised you from the Care Home brochure, and couldn't walk by without saying thank you for helping to raise funds for The Foundation.'

Jo suddenly understands what the man is referring to. The care home supported a different charity yearly. Jo had gone above and beyond in her efforts to boost the success of this year's fundraising push. For a start, she'd invited people from her 'Lawn Mowers 1950 to 1975' appreciation society to bring along mowers for a demonstration and parade on the care home lawns. The residents had been delighted to see these vintage machines so lovingly restored, and had dug deep into their pockets in financial appreciation. She also invited her facebook friends from the group 'Lanyards Through the Ages' to the home, to exhibit some of their favourite examples and share the history of them. Altogether, Jo's efforts raised £7000 for The Foundation, which Jo vaguely understood championed human rights globally.

'I'd like to thank you properly' said the man. 'Apologies for interrupting your supper, but we're about to serve a drinks and canapé reception on our lawns for Foundation supporters, will you join us?' he asked, gesturing to the large riverside residence adjacent.

Jo was momentarily silent, but her friends answered for her with a resounding yes. Arriving on his lawns, tables laid with a sumptuous buffet greeted them.

'Please meet my wife Amal, and sorry, I haven't introduced myself. I am George and together we run the Clooney Foundation for Justice. Your help has been so much appreciated Jo. Now, tuck in and enjoy the party.'

Jo wasn't completely happy about her chips and mushy peas going cold, but decided to try and enjoy the party anyway. After all, declining the invitation might possibly have made her seem rather dull.

Mike Daws

The Dinner Party

The night had just begun and everybody was taking their seats. This Dinner Party had been in the planning stages for a long time now. Lots of faces gathered round a large circular table who hadn't seen each other for years. A school reunion for want of a better word. The waiter attends the table and takes everybody's orders. The first person to speak up was a tall lady with Ginger hair...

"Hi everybody, for those of you who don't remember me I'm Trisha. I used to be in Mr. Barkers form group. I'm a influencer on Instagram now. You may have seen some of my many restaurant posts online. In fact I'm live streaming this event right now, Say Hi Guys!" A few people let out a small groan in response.

Next to speak is a short man with thick Black glasses...

"Hi folks. I'm Terry. I used to work in the Library at lunch times and run the after school games club. I'm a Police Constable now."

Then a lady with long blond hair joins the chat...

"Hello everyone. I'm Emily. I used to be in Miss Davenports form group. I'm a Director for the charity 'Mind' now."

Next up is a Large gentleman with a goatee Beard...

"Hi, I'm Kevin and I was in Mrs Ashleys form. I used to take the Register to the office every morning."

The last few of the assembled guests finish introducing themselves and the waiter arrives at the table with everybody's food orders. The last to be served is Trisha...

"This is a Special dish for you Trisha!" Beams the waiter.

Trisha grins a large smile. Her phone still live streaming to her avid viewers.

"Wow, did you hear that viewers? A Special dish for me!"

The waiter takes the large metal covering off the dish and presents it to Trisha. She moves the phone closer so her watchers get a better look. Her face turns white.

"What's this?" She Stutters.

In front of her is bowl of offal with a note attached. It Reads - Trisha Wilton - School Bully of the Year 1988"

"Don't you recognise me Trisha?" The waiter exclaims.

"No" Trisha replies Meekly.

"Take a closer look, let your audience see. Let them hear the truth. You really don't recognise me do you. Mind you I have lost a lot of weight since we last met, that time you pushed me down the stairs at school. Does the name George Morgan ring any bells?" Trisha's face turns red as a beetroot.

"Well, do you have anything to say? I organised this reunion. Everyone around this table has been hurt in some way or other by you and your cruel ways. We wanted to show everyone what you are really like. I do hope your viewers are liking the show and enjoy watching you receive your 'Just Desserts!"

George grabs Trisha's phone and addresses her followers... "Thanks for watching - Goodnight!"

Heather Suart

The Dinner Party

When the invitation arrived I was tempted to it ignore but it was from my new boss. I was rather stunned that he had invited me to his 50th party, especially as I had only been working for him for one week.

I read the first line of the invitation.

You are cordially invited to attend a dinner party to celebrate my 50th birthday on ....

I hardly knew anyone I worked with least of all my new boss. I wanted to refuse.

There was no mention of dress code. When one is cordially invited surely that means posh doesn't it? Oh crumbs, what should I wear, my wardrobe consisted of jeans, leggings, jumpers, t-shirts and a couple of suits for work. I'd have to splash out on a new dress

I bought myself a new dress and some ridiculously high heeled shoes hoping I wouldn't have to walk too far in them in fear of breaking my neck!! Now the next dilemma, a present. Flowers, wine or chocolates. Why on earth was I fretting over something so trivial.

Finally the day was here and I arrived at the venue with no mishaps.

I tottered along trying to keep upright on my new heels and rang the door bell waiting for it to be answered but to no avail. Oh crikey, had I got the wrong house. I checked the invitation again and no I had the right address.

Just as I was thinking about turning tail and leaving, someone appeared around the corner. 'Are you here for the party'? 'Yes I am', I replied, thinking what a daft question as here I am holding the invitation dressed up to the nines!

'We are round the back' was the answer. 'Come and join us'.

It appeared that a bbq was in progress with people drinking beer and cola. Embarrassingly they were all in jeans, leggings and t-shirts. Oh my, I was so overdressed. Goodness knows how my shoes would fare on the grass. I spotted my boss, with a woman, walking towards me. 'How lovely you could come' the woman said, with a beaming smile. 'My husband has told me so much about you and what a wonderful PA you are'.

'Really?' I replied somewhat overwhelmed. 'I do love your dress' she said, and whispered, 'at least someone has made the effort'. 'Just kick your shoes off if you want, the grass is very dry.' My boss took my arm. 'Come on there are so many people I want you to meet.'

'Happy birthday' I said giving him the bottle of champagne I had bought , in a moment of madness.

'Ooh lovely' he remarked. 'Just what we need to crack open for my celebration, instead of boring beer.' 'You and me are going to work well together.'

I started to relax and walked towards what I hoped would be my new friends and many more invitations.

Just a note to myself. Remember to check the dress code!!

Diane Newman

The Dinner Party

Alice stood back and looked at the dining table. She had thought of everything: a freshly pressed tablecloth, garden flowers in jam jars, candles in cut glass holders, their best wine glasses. The aquilegia flowers provided a vivid contrast to the white tablecloth. She smiled to herself at the significance of it. The scene was set. Tonight was the night.

Her husband Grant appeared in the kitchen. He looked smart, as always. His style and smile had been one of the first things that had attracted her to him. But she couldn't think about that now. 'What are we eating tonight, love?' he asked. 'Oh, well what I've prepared is best served cold' Alice said. Grant looked a little puzzled but at that moment the doorbell rang. Their guests had arrived: her best friend Kara and her husband Harry.

Alice saw a look pass between Grant and Kara. Alice noticed the slight blush that followed. 'Poor Harry, she thought, he hasn't got a clue.'

'Let's take our places' said Alice, and led them into the dining room where she uncorked a bottle of wine that was chilling in the cooler. She poured everyone a glass of the crisp white.

Kara said 'let's have a toast, it's been a while since we've seen each other.' 'Has it?' thought Alice to herself, 'some of us have been seeing a lot of each other.' She briefly thought back to the moment she had realised the devastating truth.

'Oh yes' said Alice. 'Let's have a toast- to me. To my new life'. She looked across at Kara and Harry. Harry looked puzzled. Kara's eyes had a look of panic in them. 'You see' she continued, now looking straight at Grant, 'I know what's been going on.' She reached into the back pocket of her trousers and carefully laid the mobile phone on the table. The phone that he didn't think she knew he possessed. So many messages and calls, so many clandestine meetings, for so long. 'You really should have hidden this better.' 'So- you're leaving. Tonight. In fact, you can go now'

Turning to Kara, she added, 'you're welcome to him.'

Donna Ripley

The Dinner Party

Flouting tradition, there was in fact no dinner eaten at the dinner party. The "party" arrived in convoy at A&E.

Felicity
My husband, Tristan, forgot to mention the Dinner party I was to cater that evening. I enlisted the help of my neighbour Marissa, who valiantly produced both a soup starter and some annoying positive thinking clichés!

Marissa
"Knock, knock, it's meeee! Grab some mint. I'll get the soup started. We've got this!"

Tristan
I arrived home unexpectedly early, startling my wife to such a degree that she ended up wearing the bright green pea soup starter

Nigel (Felicity's brother)
Seb's driving was insane, careening all over the road and obliterating the speed limit. I remember the grinding of metal, and simultaneously seeing sparks in my peripheral vision. I regained consciousness in A&E.

Sebastian (Nigel's partner)
I was driving carefully and well within the speed limit, when we were blindsided by another vehicle. The car tipped like a top, and rocked like a rocking horse. I'm told that I

hyperventilated to such a degree that I regained consciousness in A&E.

Felicity
We were in the bathroom cooling my miraculously only slightly scalded leg, when Tristan evaporated for some while to order takeout. Marissa sprinted to the window upon hearing the doorbell. Wilbur (our Labrador) ran to defend his territory. Marissa was upended, and plummeted out of the window. The last I saw of her was her toes. I must have banged my head when I slipped on the drenched bathroom floor trying to rescue her. Marissa and I both regained consciousness in A&E.

Piers (Tristan's boss)
On arrival, we were met with the sight of someone ahead of us being hit full force by what appeared to be a petite dark-haired woman, wearing an extremely bright floral print maxi dress, apparently flinging herself out of the first story front window. My expectant wife was induced into labour by the shock, and her waters broke. I was unable to calm her resultant hysteria and called an ambulance, only to be told that an ambulance had already been dispatched to this address. I slithered sideways on the drenched paving, and regained consciousness in A&E, a father.

Penelope Piers' wife
Despite being overwrought, I birthed a radiantly healthy baby boy, eight pounds and seven ounces. We named him Edward, after

Eduardo the pizza delivery man. Piers was pushing for Pepe (short for pepperoni) but, well, that would just be ridiculous - even if pizza saved lives that fateful night. Eduardo and Marissa are dating. Nigel and Sebastian are on honeymoon in the Bahamas, and Sebastian is seeking employment as a chauffeur. Nigel and Felicity have sworn to never cater a dinner party again, but they do have everyone from that night round for pizza once a month, with a 10% staff discount courtesy of Eduardo. Felicity never wore pea green ever again, despite living long enough to resemble a crumb in a chair.

Jennifer de Grey

The Dinner Party

Jane rose to her feet, slowly, carefully, suppressing her instinct to wince less it show any weakness. Her guests' heads turned as this very act and the manner in which it was delivered, commanded their full attention. Our Octogenarian, plus six days, hostess had a spoon poised to tap on her glass of Chardonnay. It was not, however, required. Gone were the days of lavish parties to celebrate such grand occasions such as she had put on for her mother's 80th some 40 years ago. Her son and I, the only ones present that remembered those do's the others could only imagine.
Too proud to ask for help to throw her own, she instead invited friends and family to four small individual dinner parties. This, she claimed, was all she could manage these days. However, still a sumptuous, impeccably presented feast. This was the penultimate of them.
Having seated each guest punctually at 2, tutting my apologetic arrival at 2.05pm, after 70ish miles, Jane went on to announce each invitee.
"This is Pat, a neighbour from across the road,"
Ah, I realised, Pat comes in to feed the cat when Jane is on one of her many trips away.
Cheery hellos followed.
"Trish, another neighbour from the corner," pointing unnecessarily in that direction.
Oh yes, the eccentric, whose husband, a foreign diplomat, was murdered some 40 years ago.

Our gossips were beginning to fit the faces.
"Diane,
was knocked off her feet in Waitrose by a would be shoplifter given chase by security, breaking her pelvis in four places! We had discussed at length who should be sued.
 and Mickey from next door."
"My son, Les, who you all know,"
whose loud, brash, course and painful attempts at humour had already cringed out the other diners before they'd even opened their napkins.
"Fliss, from Art Class"
new to the area and taken under Jane's wing.
"Big John, also from Art Class,"
wasn't particularly big, joined to kickstart his social life having lost his wife last year.
"My friend, Kate,"
Me. Probably gossiping later why her son's ex-live-in-lover was still on the scene and whose continued friendship with Jane he and his two previous wives since, tolerated.
Big John whispered, "that was my wife's name." Awkward. I invited him to call me Kathrine "if it made it easier,"
"and finally, Little John, Les's friend,"
who, so eager to please everyone and be 'helpful,' went on to knock planters over, wine down Jane's blouse, food unnecessarily moved about to make it "easier for everybody," all our internal voices begging that he just sit down.
"Now," Jane exclaimed, "This will be 'The Last Supper' as it were. I won't be doing any more of these," …pause for effect, her guests exchanging worried glances.
What on earth was she going to say? Minds raced. Was she ill? Was the cat ill?
No, much worse!

"I shall be expecting YOUR invitations from now on!"

A culinary arena and a test of friendships loomed.

Chris Caudron

The Dinner Party

A dinner party, a best friend coming. What could be nicer? Lamb roasting, and me cutting slices of onion and potatoes into perfectly uniform slices for the *pommes boulangères* – and meticulously removing the ones stained with blood from my cut finger.

No usual dinner party, no usual best friend either. Jan stole my husband forty-five years ago. Oh, he was willing, their appetites matched. We'd giggled through pregnancy classes, had babies together, danced with other friends' husbands at notorious seventies parties. But there it ended, I thought.
I am tinkering again with the table setting, the tulips, the cushions. The double pain was fierce. I left with a three year old son and a toddler, fled to become a waitress for the summer at my mother's hotel miles away, promising his mother I'd return in the autumn when he'd sorted out his life, his drinking, gambling – and Jan.
It's cheesecake. Jan and husband had come to dinner, we'd just met. A nervous housewife, I'd made my first cheesecake, elaborately decorated with piped cream and tangerine segments. I went to cut it but couldn't, and ran tearfully to the kitchen, scooped off the decoration and realised I'd piped over the greaseproof tin-liner. We laughed.

Serving English breakfasts made me retch, no periods – I'm pregnant! I kept my promise and returned in October, the kids would all be born in the same hospital and my second daughter appeared almost painlessly. Only one visitor came, not one I expected, to tell me that the family and my friends had been told she was not my husband's but another man's child. A disgrace back then. Only DNA would absolve me years later.

My son liked cheesecake. He died in New York aged 49, intestate and unmarried. My former husband made himself executor, had a heart attack and became demented. So for a year Jan and I have dealt with lawyers and bumf and hard decisions. The necessary conversations have been interspersed with reminiscences, accusations, lies – truths. In closer moments we talked of a reunion. She'd seen more of my son over the years than me. No longer adulteress and still with her wealthy husband, she offered her spare flat near an airport when he visited from the US. And boys forgive fathers anything it seems.

I'll serve the Campari and orange that forty seven years ago we were drinking in the garden when Jan went into premature labour. I drove her to hospital, only just fitting my own belly behind the steering wheel. It was a C-section. I would visit her tiny, hairy son in the neonatal unit while she recovered, and our babies were christened together at St Boniface church.
The salads are finished when the doorbell rings. Pinny off, smile on, I open the door, scared. Two very old, wrinkled people are standing on the doorstep. One is holding a bunch of tulips, the other's blank eyes are

elsewhere. Jan and I rush to each other's arms. The man we shared is nothing. The man we loved is dead.

Yvette P. Rejuso

The Dinner Party

Through the brittle glass doors of the house, I heard a woman's soothing voice inviting me to come out of my room. "Come dear, while the pot is hot.".
I was eight since I loathe parties. However, this evening, they say, was different.
 "Dear, your sister would be sad if you don't go out there". It wasn't the party that I hated; it was watching strangers over a constructed compact space leaving people to interact inevitably. I appreciate every individual's effort to travel from their home and gather tonight but I would have to pass on this opportunity to make friends and would rather be lying on my bed reading a book with a blanket keeping me warm. After a brief moment, I glanced at the large cloud-wavy mirror hanging above my study table. I fixated my eyes on the skin of my face which seemed to be 'glowing'. A bold-vampy red lipstick was applied on my plump and full lips, yet, I was not amused by this. They said it would only be for this night and they promised to not let me wear makeup ever again which is why I wholeheartedly agree and engage myself in meeting people at this event with a glamourized look.
Only about four steps forward, my nose sensed a passionate fragrance. Perhaps, a symphony of; a daring floral scent, a burst of sweet honey, a lingering enticing blend of strawberry and pear, a blooming lilac and rose accented with almond and cream, and an exotic green moss.

Such mouthwatering fusion evokes nothing but a delicious-vibrant scent. A fragrance, so heavy, so tempting, my feet stopped. I fixed my gaze on our backyard. Tonight's party looked classy. A unique decoration idea with a stunning floral arrangement. People seemed so alive. They had that smile; a smile reflecting sincere joy and comfort. I hesitated and started to feel edgy. Then, I saw my mother taking cheerful steps towards me. "Hi, my little dear Nadia. Come sit with us on the table.", she calmly said. "Sure, ma.", I replied. On the table, varying Italian dishes were served; Chicken Parmesan, Cacio E Pepe Chicken, Homemade Lasagna, Stromboli, Pasta Alla Gricia, Antipasto Salad, Shrimp Scampi, Burrata Salad, and Carbonara Pizza. Hungry, I gobbled each of them.

While I was chewing the lasagna my mother made, the doorbell on the gate rang. "Nadia, my dear, why don't you go meet the guest who just arrived?", my father asked. With my bitty legs, I ran to our front yard to open the gate. As fast as I could, without any worry, I opened it. Soon, regretted it.

"God! No! What happened? Hospital, we need to go to the hospital! Open your eyes! Stay with us.". I heard my mother's trembling voice. Then, the sound of something crashing was all I heard.

I wish I could have that dinner party one last time and not spend my nights in their tombs.

Rebecca Clifford

After the Wolf Blood Moon

This is a season of crisp and crackle,
layers of ice, snow, dead things,
the cries of crow and grackle.

Small creatures hide and hope for spring
while wind prods, pushes frosty
layers of ice, snow, dead things
as if to tell she's in charge, haughty.
A keen sweep of time, all surrounding,
while wind prods, pushes frosty
air; our candles in the dark, guttering,
our dreams dragged seaward, with the tide,
a keen sweep of moon, all surrounding
into a place where hope cannot abide.
How can it be so cold, so cruel?
Our dreams dragged seaward with the tide
provide this frigid hell with fuel.
This is a season of crisp and crackle.
How can it be so cold? So cruel,
the cries of crow and grackle.

Sarah Wooler

The Moon

When I look at the moon and search for you
I wonder do you see me too?
You left one day and never came back
So sudden so quickly,
You were gone and that was that.
Yet when the sun goes down and the moon comes up,
The gap is bridged and for a few stolen moments I miss you less.
The moon holds our memories
The craters are the pools of the tears shed of our loss.
When I look at the moon and search for you
I wonder do you see me too?
You left one day and never came back
So sudden so quickly,
You were gone and that was that.
Yet when the sun goes down and the moon comes up.
I remember that to be loved , love comes sometimes with loss.

Debbie Milner

The Reflecting Moon

Looking out of my window on life.
Peeping, peering through my last gap of
sunlight.
I stare up at the New Moon remorseful,
for all the extra time I should have spent with
loved ones.
'Gone,' now and forever, there is a pang in my
heart.

Suddenly I feel a moonlit glow!
Warming my soul, my whole body tingles.
It is like 'Changing Pale Faces,' smiling down
on me.
Comforted at last I experience peace.

As my time on earth is short now…
I must live it to the full.
At last I see what lies ahead with new eyes.
As a new day begins and the moon disappears
from the sky.

Heather Suart

The Moon

Moonbeams dance in the darkening skies
Stars shining brightly till dawn starts to rise
As darkness falls the moon is aglow
It's light shining bright on the world below

Serene and white this sphere stands alone
It's secrets of life still to us unknown
But one thing's for sure as time passes by
This celestial body will remain in the sky

Jennifer de Grey

Moon

Earth's only satellite
Just one second away at the speed of light
Mercury has none, they'd be destroyed by the sun
Venus's Zoozve is a sort of quasi one
Mars has two, Deimos and Phobos
Pluto had five but this 'dust cloud' is now lost
Jupiter has more than 85 that we know
Including Europa, Ganymede, Callisto and Io
Saturn with 196 has huge Titan, Rheas and Dione
Uranus' 27 include Titania, Miranda and Oberon
Neptune's Triton, Hippocamp and 14 more
Are all water deities of Greek folklore.
Our moon controls the time, the tides and the seasons too,
"Hey planets, what do your moons do for you?"

Teresa Fowler

Moon

It waxes and wanes
(whatever that means)
and of adjectives it has no dearth
though 'tis only a rock,
a mere chip off the old block
that we call Earth

By its silvery light, the cow took flight,
the cat fiddled, farmers harvested their crop
and smugglers raked its reflection,
so that revenue men couldn't catch them on the hop.

And by rhyming with so many words,
such as June, spoon, swoon or croon
that rock's saved many a poet's sanity,
thus preventing profanity.
So, here's to our moon, which has little gravity
rather like this piece of levity!

Donna Ripley

Moon

Ethereal enigmatic Mother
Favour us with your shimmering luminescence
Watch over and protect your children
Seated in celestial suspension
Understated power masked
By apparent gentle benevolence
Abeyance manipulated not forced
Changeable, malleable, inconsistent
Mysterious and multi guised Matriarch
Disappearing, hidden, vigil abandoned
All dissolves, swallowed by shadow
Enveloped into disingenuous night
Round faced Mothers return
Regurgitates all emerging from inky black
Until we sense the harsh glare
Of Father and faun for his approval
Farewell spherical countenance
Father is appeared now
His intense carcinogenic gaze
Is adored and feared in equal measure

Rebecca Clifford

I See the Moon

and, o, how I wish I could fly
free and unfettered; high,
so high, light as ether,
insubstantial as candy floss,
evasive, promising as the kiss of a butterfly,
translucent wings of gossamer, opalescence.
Shimmering opals, raindrops of love.
Love, warm, succulent, mouthwatering love,
love warmth of a love quilt on a winter's night.
A night so cold, a sky so sharp,
the darkness so deep,
stars are swallowed whole, and
only the moon cannot be conquered,
its moon ring pulsing
with moon milk.

And, o, I see the moon.

Rebecca Clifford

I See

Orion through the bedroom window.
He's here for hunting season.

Orion always makes a clean kill
pure, simple, direct to the heart
of the hart, which falls
      heroically
tragically
      dramatically
perfectly on leaves that have foretold,
in glorious gold and bronze, his demise.

Onto this leafy carpet flows the alizarin of the
hart's life's blood,
honouring the hunter as the hunter honours
him.

Orion mounts the night sky, sees the moon,
sees me through the bedroom window,
and we know that autumn has come.

Sue Ribbons

Moon

In the sky an opaque sphere
So far away yet looks near
Waxing and waining
Shiny and bright
Appearing at nighttime
Like a shadow in broad daylight

What matter makes it their abode?
Is there really an answer untold?
The going down of the moon shows us there is another day,
Individual adventure coming our way.

Then it rises lazily in the dark endless abyss
Reflecting on the silk sheet of sea with a kiss
As it tip toes silently across the night
Illuminating an owl in its forest flight

Poetry is a voice telling us we are not alone in this world
The moon is there, secrets not yet unfurled
Creating shadows in the dark without a whisper
Sometimes days of nothing, jet sky, we've missed her

There is an offing where the sky meets the sea
What lies there is our reason to be
A passive silence, a moment of thought
As clouds glide by, the moon gets caught

A mystery to conquer man has tried
A conspiracy of landing, has man lied?
Some things are richer being left in galactic splendour
Let the moon be alone her magic to tender…

Mike Daws

Moon

(The Man in The Moon)

This is The Story of The Man in The Moon,
Who is Big and Round Like a Ginormous Balloon,
Thousands of Miles Above The Earth, He Spins Around and Around,
When It's Light He Falls Asleep and Doesn't Make a Sound,
One Day A Ship Came Passing By,
It Landed Right Between His Eyes,
Out Stepped A Little Green Man,
Tall and Thin, His Name Was Sam!
Pointy Ears and Pointy Toes, Two Eyes, A Mouth, But No Nose,
The Two Became Friends and Now Live Together,
They Talk and They Talk For What Seems Like Forever!
Now The Man in The Moon Has A Man On The Moon,
If It's Dark Outside, You'll See Them Soon.
Goodnight - Sleep Tight!

Chris Ralls

Moon

I am the Moon, Earth's silent satellite,
treading the dark vacuum you call Space.
I move your restless oceans, govern your tides,
but I am free of all your worldly noise.

I have been mute for millions of years,
listening, observing your tumultuous planet.
I am not ruffled by some rushing wind;
I have no surging seas, cascading waves,
no rustling leaves or waving wheat,
no squawking birds or howling animals.
And most of all no raucous human voices,
no sounds of strife, of guns, or bombs or war.

But you upset my ageless meditations
by sending men in one of your contraptions.
Their feet disturbed dust that had lain untrodden
since I was created.
For the first time I heard a voice proclaiming
triumphantly
your victory. 'A giant step for Man'.
But I was vanquished, never the same again.

And now I fear you humans will return,
build bases for your bustling business,
carve crevices in craters,
trawl my untrammelled surface with your
tractors.

Oh, if you must come, why not bring your dead,
for they at least would not disturb my peace.
Instead of your ceaseless activity, leave me alone,
and make your parting gift a cemetery.

Loraine Banks

Moon

Moon, o Moon
A pearl in the night sky
A precious gem
For poets to ponder nigh.

Should we try to reach you
All your secrets to unfold?
Or let you keep your mystery
As it were in the days of old.

Why not leave the beautiful lady
To keep her secrets still
Allow the romance to remain
For writers to wax at will.

Man has encroached your surface
To explore for chemicals anew
But nothing fresh for humankind
Only specimens for boffins to view.

So let us leave her in peace
Her joyful magic intact
For lovers to sing about.
Not peddle in needless fact.

For lovers to sing about
As they have for eternity
To gaze upon your beauty
In perpetuity.

Diane Newman

Poem 'Moon'

You hang in the sky
A white disc glowing in Spring
Fox cubs tumble and play
Under your luminescent light;

Come Autumn
Owls call and hunt
Beneath a radiant orange sphere
Illuminating the harvest fields

Chris Caudron

Moon

The morning light was white
and blinding and suspiciously
innocent, though any fool could
see that during the night the
wind had been buffeting the last
clinging foliage from the childish
trees,

Paving the streets with gilt and
berries in
homage to the perigee
supermoon above that had
laughed from the black sky, the
biggest since the year I was born
that busy baby-sitting - I forgot
to see.

Catford, London 15th November
2016

Leanne Pilbeam

Moon Cheese

We sent a rocket to the Moon
It had a pocket for a spoon
And a little hole for forks and knives
And a flower bed full of herbs, like chives.

Plates and bowls and cups abound
Salt and pepper floated round
Of course we needed crackers too
And graters, and stuff for fondue

We whooshed, then landed safe and sound
We put our blanket on the ground
Dug with our spoon and what should come?
Moon cheese, moon cheese, moon cheese! YUM!

Bohhdan Rafalskyi

My Pet

My pet

Thick streamlined hair
Fluffy and scruffy.
You always need a dog there,
Fetching a ball, breath is huffy.

But when resting on
somebody's lap,
There's no waking him up
from his nap.
And when he's angry, the
furious bark,
Gives you the creeps
when you're in the dark.
A dog always needs to be
satisfied,
So you should've thought
when you applied.
TO HAVE A DOG

Sebby Smith (aged 6)

My Pet

My pet is a dragon
He is small and black
He has massive yellow eyes
And spins along on his back

At the top of the garden
In a deep pond he swims
Jumping out of the water
With a flap of his wings

We feed him dolphins
As a little snack
He snaps his jaws
Like a shark 'ack ack'

He can break bones
With one big bite
But he loves a story
And a cuddle at night

His secret weapon
Is frills that are grey
They make him look bigger
And scare predators away.

Ned Rollo (aged 10)

On the Beach

Jack was on the beach watching the waves lash against the rocks like a whip. Suddenly something caught his eye, it was a horn half buried in the sand. He picked it up and saw that it had blue markings around the edges. Unexpectedly, it started to glow, a bright light shone around him, and he rose into the air. Then he slumped to the ground. After a few hours Jack came around and realised the horn must have some source of power. He found himself in a small cave, and could still smell the salty sea air. He looked around, and saw stalactites stuck in the ceiling like spears. In the ground were precious stones glittering like jewels. Jack saw the horn poking out of some rubble, it was glowing again. He noticed that it had writing on it: 'The heart of the ocean'. Jack picked it up, and immediately felt an urge to walk outside into the bright, scorching sunshine. He took the horn and blew it, and a roaring foam erupted from the ocean, and it parted. Jack walked into the foaming slush and the water closed in behind him, and he had became a merman.

George Rollo (aged 10)

On the Beach

Roger loved visiting the beach, with its golden sands and lush water. For him, it was his quiet place, somewhere to go whenever he felt angry or frustrated, because it made him feel calm. One day he found a cave with a rock pool in the centre. The ceiling had tiny holes in it which filtered out the light onto the water and reflected it like a disco ball. He felt like doing a bit of exploring, and climbed over the jagged boulders, slipping and sliding on seaweed. Suddenly he slipped and tumbled down into a dense cavern. There was a bright luminous glow, and he realised it was made by fireflies swarming around the cavern. Roger turned back and looked upwards. The hole he had fallen down was too high up to climb and the slope was too steep to even attempt to climb up. Then he noticed that the fireflies were going in one direction, and he decided to follow them. He suddenly saw daylight. He had come home at last, and a warm glow ran through his body.

Harry Saunders (aged 10)

On the Beach

Once upon a time in the Kingdom of Crabs in the mill pond at the Isle of Wight 2023, 26th July, the tide was coming back in and the Kingdom of Crabs was in peace until the crab nets came down. They came down every year. Some are stupid and go into the net, but some are smarter and stay hidden under the rocks. Big and small go into the nets. It's funny watching them go into the bucket because the humans donk them around a bit. About 100 came out the pond today.

I got picked up by a human today and I nipped them. The King Crab says to never fall for the bacon but some still do and the King and Queen tells them off. It is very funny when they fall off the bridge back into the water. The King says he doesn't want anyone else to be caught. But no matter what he says, crabs will still be caught at the mill.

Maggie Jakins

Plugged In

'Cup of tea, love?' Geoff called up to his wife. 'Are you awake?'
He climbed the staircase, carefully balancing the teacups on the plastic tray, trying hard not to soak the two biscuits.
'There's a message on my phone, forgot to charge it up. I could see it flashing all night,' he grumbled, getting back under the duvet and handing Carol a tea-soaked Digestive. 'It's only a voicemail thingy from that company that does holiday insurance for what they call their silver customers.'
Carol hauled herself up on the pillow. 'Oh okay, that's because I spoke with them yesterday about that all-inclusive hotel you said you fancied. I lost patience in the end though,' she said. 'The girl had the cheek to ask if I knew which buttons to press on the phone, and was I able to open the email she was about to send? Just because they deal with people over sixty... I was using a mobile when she was still in primary school…still got it somewhere.'
Geoff chuckled, thinking it better to change the subject. 'The kids were wondering what we wanted for our anniversary next month?'
'What did they have in mind?' Carol was on a roll now. 'A CD of wartime music?'
'They don't use CDs anymore, love, everything's downloaded or uploaded or something,' Geoff said. 'Have to keep remembering to charge stuff up though.'
'Oh yes, so it is,' Carol said, taking a sip of her now lukewarm tea. 'And stored on a cloud

apparently, which actually sounds quite nice, although you won't find what you're looking for, ever again. I wanted to watch a film the other night, but Sarah said I have to stream everything these days, you can't just turn the telly on and choose your programme from the TV Times. And you can watch all episodes of a programme before they've even been on the telly!'

'You're right, it's such hard work.' Geoff put his empty teacup on the bedside table. 'On Friday night, all I wanted was to watch the gardening programme, but a message kept coming up on the screen saying I needed to log back into my service provider, enter a four-digit code and reset my PIN number,' he said. 'By the time I'd found my glasses and the right buttons on the handset, another message said I'd been logged out as I'd taken too long…and by then it was bedtime.'

Carol looked up from her empty cup. 'Shall we just book the holiday for our anniversary and disappear somewhere? Think I can just about find my way around the website…'

'That's not a bad idea,' Geoff said. And we won't be taking any mobiles, tablets, e-readers, cameras, smarty-pants watches or anything that needs charging up. We're going technology-free.'

Pam Robinson

Where next......?

I started as a seed, drifted down to the ground amid other fully grown trees. After many years I had grown into an impressive, although I say it myself, tree. I used to talk to the other trees around me, speculating on our destiny. One day we heard an unwelcome sound, that of chain saws. They were approaching, with their accompanying team of lumberjacks, across our little forest.

It hurt a bit when I crashed to the ground, and my journey to the timber yard was less than comfortable. However, when I went through the sawmill it felt wonderful, as I was slimmed down to slender strips of wood. I had to lie in a pile with other strips for about two years, to "season" me, I heard them say. Eventually I was made into a very grand dining table, with a highly polished finish, and some of my other bits were carved into very shapely legs for me to stand on.

I was moved into a family home, I think they were quite wealthy, and for many years I was cherished, polished, dusted and generally well cared for. Alas, when the children came along, and were growing up, I can only describe my fate as "being abused". Eventually, I found myself being thrown, quite unceremoniously, into a large container at the local Council tip. Before too much other stuff had landed on top of me, I felt some hands grabbing my legs. What a reprieve! I am not sure where I would have ended up if I had been crushed in that container.

After a journey in the back of a truck with some other pieces of furniture, I saw us pull into a long drive, at the end of which was a large barn, with two very high wooden doors. The driver got out of the truck and hauled open the doors and we drove in. Someone else appeared and between them they lifted me off the back of the lorry and placed me alongside a pine dresser. My rescuer and his colleague then disappeared into a large farmhouse nearby. It was a bit dark, but I could make out in the gloom, some wardrobes, two more tables, another dresser and a set of shelves. I hesitantly broached a conversation with my new found friends, and soon learnt that whatever comes in here, goes out again looking really great, although sometimes, very different. Apparently my saviour was in to, what they called, "up-cycling". I was there for about two weeks, during which time I saw the pine dresser disappear, only to return as a table and two stools. Getting rather excited, waiting for my turn, I wondered what on earth would this magician do with my ink-stained table top, that was dented with countless impressions from ballpoint pens.

My turn came and firstly I was dipped into a warm bath, then scrubbed with a wire brush. Not very pleasant, the scrubbing, but it made me feel lovely and clean and fresh. My carved legs were removed and, two days later were

Gail Landon

Today Veyra Rules

Ex-army colonel Veyra Bhuktina set down the two metal buckets she had brought into the "Sapphire Market". Eighty-year-old Veyra ruled here but worried that there would be a usurper.
'Those who have served' she consoled herself, 'know I was a senior officer. 'They should still obey'.
'Odd is lucky' she muttered, counting seven, brown, paper bags full of sunflower seeds onto the smooth top of an old machine gun emplacement. She was ready to sell her seeds.
'Over we go!' she continued and tipped one of her two buckets upside down. A glued-on string cushion on the base protected Veyra's ample rear as she sat down. She felt for the ready-to-celebrate-her-next-triumph-small-vodka-bottle, hidden deep in the second bucket full of seeds. It was her only vice. Bathed in summer sunshine she observed the crowds.
Veyra's famed sixth sense made her look harder at a youth with a hessian sack-bag slung over his shoulder.
'Why is his bag wide open?' Veyra muttered. Veyra immediately stood up, stretching her arms above her head.
Felix Rublyov, an ex-army officer saw her, so hung a red sweater at the front of his 'Woollen's Stall'. Scarlet skirts, wide-ripe-red strawberries and crimson carpets were moved to prominent 'on guard' positions. In thirty seconds 'Sapphire Market' was on high alert.

The youth, completely unaware of his reception, had planned his pathway to the souvenir stall run by Elyena Ivanov, a slender blond. With a sudden move he pushed her backwards, forced his hand into the cash bag under her blouse and transferred the cash into his sack bag, then yelled in pain as he half staggered away and fell to the ground. Blood oozed
through his tee shirt. An epee hilt protruded from his back. Elyena's father, an army fencer, pulled sides of the cut canvas on his stall together again and hurried to the body whilst his wife raced to help her daughter.
In seconds Felix Rublyov had run to check the youth was dead. He removed the sack-bag and pulled out the epee, passing it to Elyena's father who stuffed it under the back of the fish stall, out of sight. Felix dragged the body under the canvas behind his own stall and covered it with a tattered tarpaulin. Witnesses looked the other way.
Veyra hurried up the slope to the scene of the crime, confident that in this down-town area no-one would report the killing. No-one ever officially saw anything.
The authorities would not be informed, and Veyra Bhuktina, the market matriarch would supervise events as she had done before, the body being thrown in one of the fast sea-going canals. The had, with the aid of those who'd served in the army and knew how to take orders, always organised action for every eventuality.
Veyra was confident she had proved herself the unrivalled market leader. How could anyone challenge her …… today?

Creative Writing Competitions - Winners

Short Story – The Dinner Party
1st Mike Daws
2nd Maggie Jakins
Highly commended - Jacky Long
Highly commended - Donna Ripley

Poetry – Moon
1st   Chris Ralls
2nd   Chris Caudron
Highly Commended - Rebecca Clifford (for3 excellent entries)

Children's entries

Short stories – On the Beach
1st George Rollo (10)
2nd Ned Rollo (10)
3rd Harry Saunders (10)

Poem – My pet
1st Sabby Smith (6)
2nd Bohhdan Rafalskyi (9)

Printed in Great Britain
by Amazon